THE
VIKING FARM

Unn Pedersen

THE VIKING FARM

Translated from Norwegian by John Hines
Illustrated by Trond Bredesen

GYLDENDAL

The original title: *På en gård i vikingtiden*
© Gyldendal Norsk Forlag AS – Gyldendal Barn & Ungdom 2013
English edition © Gyldendal Norsk Forlag 2016

Design: Gyldendal Barn & Ungdom

Photos and illustrations:
Museum of Cultural History (KHM), University of Oslo (UiO)/ photographer Eirik Irgens Johnsen: pages 10, 15 bottom, 22, 26, 46, 54
KHM, UiO/ Ellen C. Holte: pages 3, 11, 30
KHM, UiO/ Inge Lindblom: pages 2, 38
KHM, UiO/ Gaute Reitan: page 15 top
KHM, UiO, E18-prosjektet: pages 23, 39 top
KMH, UiO: page 31
The Kaupang Excavation Project, UiO: page 18
Morten Rakke: page 6
Arkikon.no: pages 14, 27 bottom, 39 bottom, 51
Kjell Ove Storvik/ Lofotr Vikingmuseum: page 19 top
NTNU University Museum/ Ole Bjørn Pedersen: page 19 bottom
Eva Andersson 2003 *Tools for textile production from Birka and Hedeby:* page 27 top
Arkeologisk Museum, University of Stavanger/ Åge Pedersen: page 34
Oluf Rygh 1885 *Norske Oldsager:* pages 35 bottom, 47 bottom
Unn Pedersen: pages 42, 43, 55
Tromsø University Museum/ Jorunn Rødli: page 47 top
Norsk Arkeologisk Selskap *Viking* 1958:192: page 35 top
Tor Bjørvik/ Hedrum historielag: page 50

This translation has been published with the financial support of NORLA and Souvenir Normand, British Section.
The author has received financial support from *Det faglitterære fond.*

Print: UAB Baltoprint, Litauen 2016

ISBN 978-82-05-49695-8

www.gyldendal.no

Contents

Facts, research and imagination

This book is about life on a farm in the age of the Vikings. Nearly everybody lived on farms at that time. That was where they spent their lives, worked, died and were buried.

What we know about the farms of the Viking Age comes first and foremost from archaeological excavations. Archaeologists uncover the remains of buildings and traces of life on the farm when they dig in the ground. They also investigate the places where people were buried. They find not just skeletons but also objects that provide information on how people lived and what they believed in. This is good, because we do not have much that was written down in the Viking Age. People did tell each other stories, all the same, and these stories were handed down from generation to

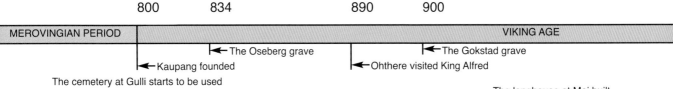

| 800 | 834 | | 890 | 900 |

MEROVINGIAN PERIOD | VIKING AGE

←The Oseberg grave

←The Gokstad grave

←Kaupang founded

←Ohthere visited King Alfred

The cemetery at Gulli starts to be used

The longhouse at Moi built

generation. Luckily, some of these stories were written down later in the Middle Ages.

I, who have written this book, am an archaeologist and I study the Viking Age. I have used my imagination and written twelve stories about two 11-year-olds' experiences on a Viking-age farm. I have imagined that this farm is situated where Hedrum church in Vestfold, Norway is today. In the churchyard there archaeologists have found a farm building and graves from Viking times.

The stories about Thora and Ravn are not purely imaginary. I have based the stories on what specialists know today. You can read about the research on the Facts pages. There are some things that we specialists are quite sure about and other things that are likely, based on what we know about the Viking Age. Specialists also disagree with each other about what is most likely.

We are constantly discovering more about the Viking Age. This can happen when archaeologists excavate new sites, or when other people – maybe you? – find objects from the Viking Age just by chance. We also get new information

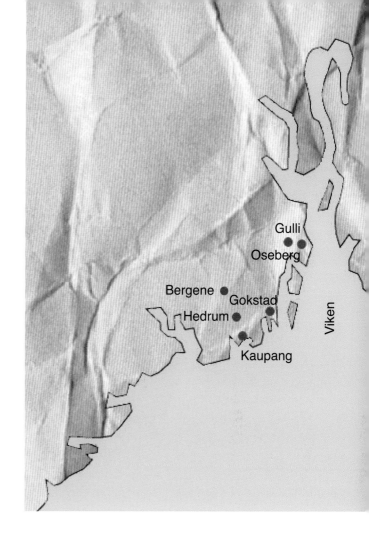

when researchers discover that they can interpret finds in new ways. If you read or hear news about the Viking Age, you can think about the stories of Thora and Ravn. Does the new information fit those stories? Perhaps you will have to modify the story I have told?

65   1050   1179

MEDIEVAL PERIOD

← Al-Tartushi visited Hedeby   ← Gunnvor raised a memorial stone   ← Snorri was born
← Harald Bluetooth raised
   a memorial stone

7

Welcome to the farm!

It is icy cold. Thora has ice in her eyelashes, and her cheeks are frozen, but a bear fur and a reindeer skin keep her body nice and warm. She loves driving in a horse and sleigh, especially when it is going as fast as it is now. They

realizes that her mother and father want to arrive before it gets dark.

Thora is looking forward to getting there! Finally she will see her cousin Ravn again. She has missed him every day since he came to visit them in the summer. In her hand she has the present she has bought for him. She knows it is something he wants!

This is the first time she has visited Ravn, and they are going to celebrate Yule together at the farm he lives on. This was where her father had been brought up and she has heard lots of stories about it. It is also the first time she has travelled such a long way from Kaupang, the town where she lives. Thora keeps looking out for the farm, but cannot see it yet. In the dusk it is hard to make out anything at all. Suddenly the sleigh turns away from the river, up a slope and into a field. She can recognize the smell of smoke from a house, but she cannot see it until the door is opened and the doorway is filled with light. First a big man comes into view and then a boy.

"Ravn!" shouts Thora, wanting to leap towards him.

"Be a bit more patient!" says her mother, holding on to her tightly. "It isn't a good idea to jump off a sleigh at full speed!"

sweep along the frozen river, and the rattles clatter and jingle. The sun has now gone below the horizon and Thora

Facts

On a sleigh across the ice

In the Viking Age, there were hardly any roads, and most journeys were made along rivers, fjords and the coast. In the summer, people would travel by boat and in the winter they used a horse and sleigh. Four sleighs were found in a large grave mound at Oseberg in Vestfold, Norway. Because of the damp clay in the grave mound, the wood of which the sleighs were made has been preserved.

One of the sleighs is simple and was probably used for carrying heavy objects around. The others are delicately carved and decorated with metal, and one was painted black and red. The sleighs from Oseberg belonged to one of the richest women in Vestfold, and they were certainly more highly decorated than the sleighs that farmers and townspeople used for their journeys.

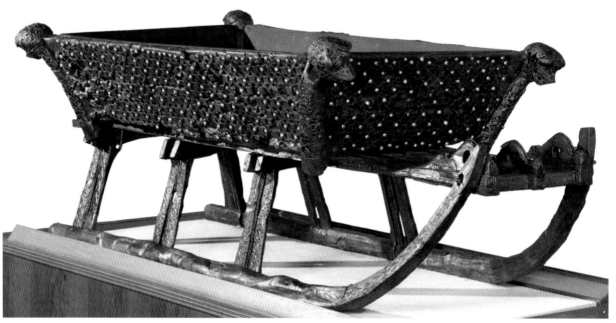

One of the sleighs from the Oseberg grave. It is on display in the Viking Ship Museum, Oslo.

Fur from wild animals

Many people used fur to keep themselves warm. In some graves bears' claws have been found; they are probably what is left of a bear's skin that has rotted away. Maybe the people who were buried in the skin believed that they could take on the bear's character and become as powerful as a bear. Some scholars think that people believed that humans could transform into animals. Was this the reason why many children were given names like *Bjørn* (Bear) and *Ravn* (Raven)?

Skins were also used to make payments. The Saami, people who lived by hunting and gathering, had to pay taxes in otter, marten, bear and reindeer skins. We know this because Ohthere, a chieftain from northern Norway, described the practice to the English king Alfred the Great. The king was so interested in the story that he had it written down.

Rattles

In some graves we find iron objects that archaeologists call 'rattles'. We have no idea what they were called in the Viking Age. A rattle consists of several rings that make a noise when they knock against each other. The rattles are often found together with horses or horse-harness. This is why some archaeologists believe

A rattle found in a grave at Gulli.

that they were fastened to the horse or the sleigh. Others have suggested that they were used to make a sound during funerals, rather like a musical instrument.

From wind-eye to window

The houses of the Viking Age did not have large windows as houses do now. However, in some walls there might have been small round holes without glass in them, a little bit smaller than your face. These peepholes are found in planks from the Viking Age. They were called *vindauga*, which means 'wind-eye', because the wind could blow right through them. After many centuries this word has turned into the word 'window'.

Guests in the longhouse

Thora races to the doorway.
"Ravn, I've missed you!" she shrieks, and leaps on him with a hug.

He's a bit embarrassed, as usual, but then he smiles and begins to laugh.

"We heard that you were coming," he says with a grin. "I don't think I've ever heard a sleigh make so much noise. You must have frightened off any evil spirits for miles around."

"Let our guests come in!" calls Aunt Ingrid. Ravn and Uncle Bjørn step aside and Thora and her parents step over the threshold.

The room is lit up by the flames from the hearth in the centre. Thora looks around her with curiosity. The house is much larger than the one she lives in, and it is also higher up to the roof. The smoke gets in her eyes, but it's nice to be inside in the warm. Above the fire a heavy iron cauldron is hanging with something in it that smells lovely.

"The food's ready, Thora," says Aunt Ingrid. "I can see you're hungry."

"Maybe you'd like to see our presents first?" suggests Thora. She opens her purse and takes out two glass beads. She gives them to Sigrid, Ravn's big sister.

"The blue one was made by the beadmaker in Kaupang and the green one is from Baghdad," she explains.

Aunt Ingrid is given a beautiful shawl, which Thora's mother has woven, and Uncle Bjørn gets a wooden bowl full of

delicious honey. Ravn looks expectantly at Thora and she has to tease him a bit.

"Now I'm looking forward to the food," she says and walks over to the cauldron. Then Ravn looks so disappointed that she quickly adds: "But first, Ravn's got to have his present!"

She pulls out a long stone that she has hidden in her mitten and puts it into his hand.

"My own whetstone!" cries Ravn, excitedly. He pulls his knife from its sheath on his belt and begins to sharpen it straightaway.

Facts

The longhouse

In the Viking Age, many people lived in what we call longhouses. These have long since rotted away, burnt down or been demolished, but archaeologists find clear traces of them. The roof of the longhouse was held up by thick posts. In order for the posts to stand firm, they were rooted in holes dug into the ground. When archaeologists find post-holes, they can see how large the building was. Sometimes they also find other remains of the house, such as the hearth, the outside walls and the interior walls.

Smokey, cold and dingy

You certainly wouldn't think it was particularly comfortable in a house of the Viking Age. There were no large windows to let the light in and no electricity. On the floor, in the middle of the largest room, there was a large, four-sided fireplace, but there was no chimney: only a hole in the roof for the smoke to escape through. This hearth provided warmth and light for those who were around it, but in the nooks and corners it was cold and dark. Archaeologists have found a few iron lamps, but only in the graves of rich

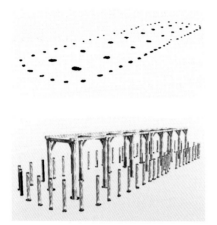

This is how archaeologists are able to reconstruct a longhouse when they have found the holes left by the posts that held the roof up.

The excavation of a longhouse at Moi in Setesdal, Norway. The archaeologists have put red and white poles in the post-holes to show how big the building was.

people. Perhaps it was only the very richest who had lamps in their houses?

Whetstones

With a whetstone you can sharpen a knife, an axe, shears or a sickle. Archaeologists often find whetstones in graves or at farms. Many of them are made of a dark and fine-grained stone that is called slate. Geologists, scientists who are specialists in stones, have discovered that the slate comes from the west coast of Norway. The slate was quarried out of the mountain and then transported by boat and sleigh all over Scandinavia.

A slate whetstone.

Houses that did not last long

In various places in Scandinavia there are wooden buildings that are many centuries old. But there is not a single longhouse, because they did not remain standing for very long. Many were probably pulled down after less than a hundred years. The posts that were sunk into the ground rotted quickly. Archaeologists can see that the posts were replaced at regular intervals. As the Viking Age went on, people began to build houses in new ways and log cabins gradually became normal. The timber was no longer rooted in the ground and this meant that the buildings would last longer. In Norway there are log cabins that were built more than 800 years ago.

The farm wakes up

Thora wakes up after the first night in the farm where Ravn lives, and wonders who is snoring so loudly.

Possibly Uncle Bjørn or Old-Ravn, the grandfather. She props herself up between the furs and peers around the dark room.

16

realizes that the slave woman is grinding grain. It must have also been she who made sure that the fire was burning.

As her eyes gradually adjust to the dark, Thora is able to make out the wall bench on the opposite side. That is where Ravn and his family are sleeping. A small shape is starting to pick itself up.

"Ravn?" whispers Thora.

Like a dart, he zips over to her. He makes a sign that she should follow him. They get dressed quickly and slip out of the door. The daylight is starting to appear. The slave is busy clearing a path to the other buildings of the farm. It must have been snowing all night.

"Do you want to come and ski around the fields?" asks Ravn. He picks out two pairs of skis and a stick for each of them. They put on the skis and go out of the farm. Ravn skis well and has to wait for Thora.

"Not fair!" she sniffs. "Wearing a dress is rubbish when you're skiing."

Ravn laughs. "Just wait," he says, "we'll be at a great hill in a minute."

The wind catches Thora's dress as she starts down the slope. She shrieks with excitement and zooms straight past Ravn. He is so surprised that he falls flat on his face, and Thora gets back to the top again first. They ski down the hill lots and lots of times.

On the bench beside her, her mother and father are fast asleep. She can hear the creaking sound from the millstone, and

Facts

Everyone slept in the same room

The longhouse had a large room in the middle of the house in which every member of the family slept, ate and did various jobs. Food was prepared in this room too. When people were eating and working indoors, they sat on the wide wall benches alongside the hearth, and they slept on them at night. There wasn't very much private life on a Viking-age farm. There is a lot to suggest that it did not matter very much for people to have their own time and space. Keeping apart from the others is treated as strange in sagas from the Middle Ages.

Millstones were used to grind grain into flour.

Bedclothes

In the graves of rich people, remains of pillows and duvets filled with feathers have been found. Farmers must also have used woollen blankets, skins and furs to keep warm at night, and straw was used as a mattress on the wall benches.

The slaves did the hardest work

The slaves were called 'thralls', and they had to do all the hardest work on the farm. There were slaves on the majority of farms, although the poorest farmers did not have slaves. Like the farm animals, the slaves were owned by the farmers and they had no control over their own lives. The farmers could sell them or kill them, if they chose to. The children of slaves were born as slaves, although it could happen that some of them were freed during their lifetime.

The extended family

Several generations lived together. Unmarried aunts, uncles, sons and daughters could also be living at the

At Borg in Lofoten a copy of a longhouse that was 83 metres long has been built. This is more than twice the length of the building at Moi shown on page 15, and is the biggest longhouse that has been found in Norway.

farm. It is difficult to know for certain how many people would usually live at one farm. There must have been more at the larger farms than at the small ones. We also do not know if the slaves were allowed to live in the longhouse or stayed in the byre with the animals.

Skiing

A picture that was scratched into the mountainside at Bøla in Trøndelag shows that there were people using skis in Norway 6000 years ago, in the Stone Age. The oldest surviving ski in Norway is more than 5000 years old and was found in a bog at Drevja in Nordland. Several thousand years later, the Viking-age king Olaf Tryggvason could boast of how good he was at skiing. In the Viking Age, people used one long ski and one short one; when they had to climb steep hills they tied fur on to one ski to get a good grip.

This ski from Drevja is now in the NTNU University Museum, Trondheim, Norway.

Work in the byre

The others have got up by the time Thora and Ravn come back from skiing. Sigrid is doing her hair, Aunt Ingrid is rolling up the bedclothes and Uncle Bjørn is standing with his head in the washtub. Over the fireplace hangs a cauldron of porridge. Thora and Ravn go up to the hearth to warm themselves. Oh, it will be lovely to have breakfast.

Thora is tired after getting up so early, but after they have eaten they all have to start work.

"We've got to hurry," says Uncle Bjørn firmly. "We must make use of the short period of daylight now that it is mid-winter."

"Can I help Ravn?" Thora rushes to ask. She would do anything at all to avoid what she always ends up with: the endless spinning. This is fine with the adults, so she gets to go out with Ravn again. They run off together to the other large building of the farm. This is the byre, Thora quickly realizes. She recognizes the pungent smell and hears the sheep bleating.

"I'm the one who's responsible for feeding the animals," says Ravn proudly. He brings out two large bundles of twigs and they start on the sheep. Thora looks around and notices some wooden cups. She goes closer and finds a child lying there, asleep in the hay.

"So this is where the slaves live," she says. "Ugh, what a snotty and ugly slave-child."

Ravn nods and passes her hay for the horses.

"That's a lovely horse," says Thora, admiringly, and she snuggles up to the largest one.

"She is well cared for," says Ravn. "Sigrid grooms her every single day."

Thora climbs up on one of the stalls and jumps down into the hay.

"Thora the Wild," says Ravn, mimicking the firm voice of Thora's mother. "Stop that and take the horses some more hay!"

Facts

Farm animals

We know what domesticated animals they had on the farms of the Viking Age because many pieces of bone have been found. Horses and oxen were used as draught animals. Cows, sheep and goats provided milk, which was drunk or made into butter and cheese. The people got eggs from chickens. They would eat the meat of all these animals and the animals' dung was used as manure on the fields.

Most things were produced on the farm

A Viking-age farm produced practically everything it needed in terms of food,

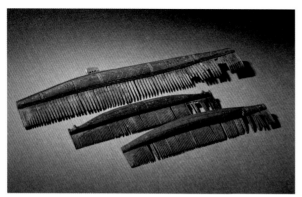

Combs for people (the two at the bottom) and for a horse (at the top).

drink, clothing, fuel and building material. It was also necessary to ensure that there was enough grain for the fields to be sown the following year. If the summer was too cold, dry or wet, there might be too little food for the winter. Then both children and adults alike had to go to bed hungry. If there were several bad years in a row, people were hungry nearly all the time and many of them would die.

Child labour

Children had to help with the work even when they were small and 15-year-olds were counted as adults. There were many simple jobs that had to be done on the farm every single day. And the children may have had the job of feeding the farm animals in the winter. The animals went out to graze in the summer season, but in the winter they were kept in the byre. So that they could survive through to the spring, there had to be enough food for them. The children could also be made responsible for gathering in branches,

A soapstone cauldron being excavated from a grave at Gulli.

leaves and heather, which were used as winter fodder. The stomach of an ox that was found in the Oseberg grave contained heather.

The fields around the farm

It was important for the farmers of the Viking Age to produce their own food. In the fields, which were usually close to the longhouse, they grew barley, wheat and oats. Farmers also grew some vegetables, such as onions, turnips, cabbages and beans.

Porridge was everyday food

Porridge was probably what was eaten most often on the farm. The porridge was made from flour and water or flour and sour milk and cooked in cauldrons carved from soapstone. Archaeologists find cauldrons like this in Viking-age graves, and pieces of broken cauldrons are often found in the ground where the farms once were. *Grjót* is the Old Norse word for stone. It is closely related to *gryte,* the Norwegian word for cauldron, and *graut,* the Norwegian word for porridge.

Combs for people and for horses

Grave finds show that many people had their own combs. The combs are made of horn and have fine patterns incised into them. Many of them are quite worn down, so they appear to have been used a lot. Some combs are so large that they would not work for people. They were used to groom horses' manes and tails.

Story time beside the loom

Thora did not get out of spinning. When they came back from the byre, she had to start. She glances at Ravn and rolls her eyes, but is careful to make sure that the grown-ups don't see. Toothless Old-Ravn grins. He saw it, but doesn't let on. He is spinning too and it doesn't look as if he enjoys it either.

"The boy can help," he suggests.

"Something sensible from old grandpa at last!" replies Aunt Ingrid, passing Ravn a spindle.

Thora notices that it is only she who has to spin slender, fine thread. She is proud that her yarn will be woven into the beautiful clothes that her mother sells in the town to rich and powerful ladies. Old-Ravn and young Ravn are spinning coarse yarn for everyday clothes.

"The two ravens…," she says out loud. "Dear Aunt, can you tell us the story of Odin's ravens?" Thora loves listening to Aunt Ingrid and her aunt loves telling the stories of the gods.

"We need to move closer to the loom," suggests Aunt Ingrid. "Then I can tell the story while the expert can weave more of my wall-hanging." She winks knowingly at Thora's mother.

"But no one gets out of spinning," says Thora's mother, looking hard at Thora and Old-Ravn.

"Every single day, Huginn and Muninn fly around the world. They see and hear everything that happens amongst people," relates Aunt Ingrid, while Thora's mother starts to weave the ravens into the tapestry. "Every evening they fly back to Odin and recount all that they have seen and heard."

Thora wonders whether Huginn and Muninn are watching her at that very moment and she glances up to the air- vent in the roof to see if she can spot them.

Facts

Clothes made on the farm

One of the most important jobs of work on the farm was making clothes for everyone who lived there. First the wool was sheared from the sheep with a large pair of shears, and then the fleece was combed with iron combs. It was spun into yarn using a hand-held spindle and this yarn was woven into material, which was sewn to make clothes. Archaeologists often find equipment for making clothes in women's graves. They therefore believe that this was the women's responsibility. A lot of yarn was needed for making clothes for so many people; children and the elderly certainly had to help with the spinning.

Stories about the gods

In the Viking Age, people believed in gods like Odin, the one-eyed god, and Freyja, the goddess of love. There were a lot of stories about the gods. We know some of them very well. They were written down several centuries later by Snorri Sturluson and other people in Iceland. Before then, people had had to memorize the stories and pass them on. We can see some of the well-known stories represented on pieces of jewellery, tapestries and picture stones from the Viking Age, but we can also see characters from stories that have not been written down.

Thor's hammer

Thor, with his hammer, was a god in whom many people believed. We know that because they used small Thor's hammers as jewellery. Many children, like Thora, were named after this god.

Thor's hammer from the Viking-age town of Kaupang.

Tapestries with pictures of the gods

In the graves of rich people, like the Oseberg grave, hangings with colourful pictures have been found. Archaeologists believe that these hung on the walls of rich people's houses. What has survived of the tapestry in the Oseberg grave is so well preserved that it is quite clear what it portrayed. We can recognize Odin's two ravens, Huginn and Muninn, for example.

Snorri Sturluson

Snorri Sturluson was an Icelandic chieftain and author who lived from 1179 to 1241. He had heard many stories that had been handed down since the Viking Age and he had read a lot of books written by others. He used this knowledge when he wrote the sagas of the Norwegian kings and *Edda,* a teaching book about poetry.

Little respect for the old?

It is not clear whether people had very much respect for the old. In *Egils saga,* the elderly chieftain and one-time

warrior Egil Skalla-Grímsson complains that he is being bullied by the women of the farm. He is also told that he is in the way when he tries to warm himself by the fire.

The spindle consists of a wooden rod, or 'distaff', and a round 'spindle-whorl' of clay or stone. The shape and weight of the spindle-whorl control how thick the yarn will be.

This is what the loom on which cloth was woven for clothing looked like. The parts that were made of wood have usually rotted away but the loom-weights, which hang at the bottom, do survive. They were made of clay or stone.

Thora learns how to weave

"That's where the tapestry will hang when it's finished," says Aunt Ingrid, pointing above the wall bench. Thora has only once before seen tapestries with pictures of the gods. That was when Ravn had come to visit her in the town. They sneaked into Skiringssal during a big party, and peeped into the queen's

feasting hall. There were incredible tapestries there.

Thora looks over at Aunt Ingrid and is aware that she has grown up with lots of tapestries like this around her. She comes from a rich and powerful family. She was married to a chieftain first. They had Sigrid together, but the chieftain was unkind and Aunt Ingrid separated from him. Later she met Uncle Bjørn and married him. They had Ravn. Thora knows that Ravn also has a grown-up elder brother. He is from her uncle's first marriage, but his mother died a long time ago. So Ravn's mother and father both already had children when they got married.

The others are sitting with their own thoughts too, because it is utterly silent in the room. After a while, Aunt Ingrid goes over to the chest by the wall. She picks out some small, square plates and gives them to Thora.

"Today, you're going to learn how to weave ribbons," she says. "At home I expect you're just spinning all day long."

Thora is allowed to choose the colours: red, pink and yellow. She watches closely while Aunt Ingrid threads the yarn through the small holes in the plates. Then she takes hold of the tablet loom and her aunt tells her what she has to do. Thora has to concentrate very hard, but she soon works it out!

"You do have a real talent!" says her aunt, with pleasure. "Perhaps you've got that from your mother, despite all your wildness!"

Sigrid goes over to the chest and gets the tablet loom she is working on. Thora thinks the pattern looks a difficult one.

"How can you remember that?" she asks.

"I've learnt a song that helps," Sigrid explains. Then she sits down with the tablet loom and begins to sing.

Facts

Learning by doing

Children did not go to school, but they learned a lot all the same. They copied what the adults did and adults showed children how to do the various jobs. The most important thing for the children to learn was practical work. When they were grown up, it would be their turn to run the farm in such a way that all who lived there would be able to have a good life.

Tablet weaving

Graves from the Viking Age sometimes contain remains of ribbons with delicate patterns in many colours. They were used to ornament dresses and capes. These ribbons were woven using a tablet loom. This sort of loom consists of thin, square wooden plates with a small hole in each corner. Some of the ribbons have extremely complicated patterns, and archaeologists have wondered how whoever made them managed to remember the patterns. One theory is that they may have sung songs with words that were repeated.

A pair of shears of iron.

Divorces

A woman could divorce her husband if he was unkind to her or her children. She could also do so if her husband was idle or treated other members of her family badly. The woman was given something of value from her home when she was married. This marriage gift was under her own control, and she kept it if she divorced.

Half-brothers and -sisters

In a family of siblings, there were often half-brothers and -sisters, and many children grew up with a step-mother or step-father. This could be because their parents were divorced or because one or both of their parents had died. There were no doctors or hospitals and many people died from illnesses that are not dangerous nowadays. Many women died during or after giving birth. Most people who lost a husband or wife, or who divorced, remarried very quickly. This was necessary for all the work on the farm to be done.

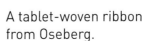

A tablet-woven ribbon from Oseberg.

31

In the logging woods

The next morning, Thora and Ravn dressed warmly, with caps and mittens. They were being allowed to follow the men into the logging woods.

"You have got to promise to be careful," their mothers insist.

"Oh, yes," they answer in chorus.

"We'll keep close to the grown-ups," says Thora.

"And keep an eye out for the falling trees," adds Ravn.

Uncle Bjørn picks out some axes, and Thora and Ravn are given one each. Ravn puts their food-pack into a rucksack.

As they go out, they see that the slave has put a harness on to the workhorse and attached the work sleigh. Thora and Ravn put on their skis, while the adults choose to go on foot.

When they reach where they have planned, each of the men begins to chop a tree down. Thora and Ravn take off their skis and go on an exploratory walk.

"Look," says Ravn, pointing down into the snow. "Both a fox and a deer have passed through here."

But Thora has found a brilliant tree for climbing and isn't interested in animal tracks. "Let's see who can get up highest!" she shouts, and points to the tree.

Ravn rushes off to another tree. They climb high up, both of them, but then Ravn gets stuck and Thora is the winner. She shouts so loud with pleasure that she could be heard for miles around. They swing on the branches on the way down and sink deep into the snow when they jump to the ground.

"Look at this," says Thora, and moves to climb up an unusual curving tree.

"No, stop!" shouts Ravn. "You're ruining my boat!"

Thora looks dumbly at him, until Ravn explains that the tree will one day be used for building a boat.

"Old-Ravn began to bend the tree using the rope you can see," he adds. "He has adjusted the rope every summer to get exactly the right shape."

Then they hear a crack and turn towards the noise. It is the first tree falling to the ground.

"Come here, children," shouts Uncle Bjørn. "Now you have to make yourselves useful by cutting the branches off this birch tree."

Facts

Woods as part of the farm

The farmers looked after their woodland well and took care that the trees grew large and strong. The trees they felled provided them with wood and material for building and repairing houses. They also made utensils such as food bowls, axe-handles, barrels, washtubs, sledges and wall benches out of wood. They picked berries in the woods and gathered winter fodder for the farm animals. In the summer the animals were pastured in the woods, eating grass, leaves and branches.

The work axe

The work axes of the Viking Age had wooden handles and iron heads, and were very similar to the axes we use today. The handle has usually rotted away, although archaeologists sometimes find small fragments of wood in the rusty iron. Both men and women could be buried with a work axe.

A biologist drills down into the bog to take a sample.

Building material for the next generation

Many people were skilled at making objects out of wood. They were particular about the material used for buildings and really wanted it to be perfectly suited to what they were making. When a boat was built, it was especially important to have material of the right shape. For this reason, some archaeologists believe that people made sure that trees grew bowed, so that the next generation would be able to build excellent boats.

Special horseshoes

In the winter, the horses had special ice-shoes, so that they would not slip on the ice and snow. These anti-slip plates were quite small and were fastened on to the horse's hooves. We know this because some of the horses that were buried have these special horseshoes on.

The rucksack

In a large grave mound at Gokstad in Vestfold, archaeologists found remains of

An ice-shoe.

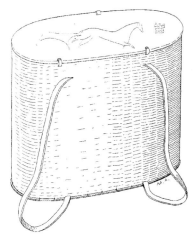

This is what the archaeologists think the rucksack from Gokstad looked like.

a rucksack made of wood and bark. Two horses and delicate patterns had been incised on the flap of the rucksack.

When the spruce arrived in Norway

Nowadays there are spruce forests in many parts of Norway, but this species of tree has not always been there. Spruces began spreading into Norway in the centuries before the Viking Age. Biologists have discovered this by studying and taking samples from bogs. Pollen, the dust that comes off flowers, falls into the bogs from the trees surrounding them. Pollen is produced every year, and it overlays the pollen from the previous year. Biologists have not found any spruce pollen in the very earliest layers in the bogs. It appears only when we are getting close to the layers from the Viking Age.

The family cemetery

They work in the woods for several hours, and are all worn out and covered with snow.

"I think we'll stop now," says Uncle Bjørn eventually. "We have to be out of the woods well before it gets dark."

The slave has already put all the logs on the sleigh and Thora and Ravn fasten their skis on.

"Follow me," says Ravn. "I'll check my traps just over here."

In each of two traps there is a dead hare and Ravn is thrilled as he takes them out.

"Now we'll have a lovely dinner," he says, "and you can have the skin."

Thora has to feel it right there and then. The fur is so soft and good, and she will have it as a collar on her cape.

Then they rush after the adults.

They take a different way back to the farm and go through the family cemetery. Thora can see the small mounds that are close together under the snow. Everyone comes to a halt.

"Your ancestors are buried inside these mounds," explains Uncle Bjørn. "And this is the grave of my mother, your grandmother," he continues, pointing to the nearest mound.

"She had a grand burial," he says. "Friends and family came from far and near. We slaughtered a horse and she was buried with much wealth, her finest clothes, beautiful jewellery and lots of vessels full of lovely food."

Ravn takes what's left of his food-pack out of his bag and places it into a wooden bowl that has been placed alongside his grandmother's burial mound; he shows her the two hares. Thora tells her about the journey to the farm and how much fun she is having.

Facts

Burial mounds

There were various ways in which the dead were buried. Some of them were laid to rest in 'barrows', and these are the graves we know most about. It is quite easy to find graves like this because they can be seen as either small or large mounds in the landscape. There are often several burial mounds together. In some places all of the mounds are from the Viking Age, but in others there may be graves that are hundreds of years older.

Graves with a lot of things in them

The dead were buried with clothes, jewellery, tools, cauldrons and pots. If it has been damp in the grave without much air, what was inside the pots may have been preserved. Archaeologists have, for instance, found bilberries and apples in pots like this. There can also be boats or sleighs in the graves. Some people were buried with one or more animals, usually dogs or horses.

Being remembered

In the Viking Age, not much was written down, but information was preserved in the stories people told each other. It was an honour to be remembered for a long time after one died. This was certainly one of the

This cemetery at Gulli in Vestfold, Norway, was discovered by an archaeologist who flew over it in a small plane. The rings in the field are the remains of burial mounds that have otherwise disappeared.

reasons why the burials were so magnificent. People were meant to talk about them for a long time.

Old stories

Some of the stories from the Viking Age continued to be told for an incredibly long time. In the twentieth century, an archaeologist started to excavate a burial mound in Trøndelag. Before he started to dig, he was told that there was a knight in the grave. The man who told him that was quite right: in the grave the archaeologist found a man of the Viking Age buried with riding equipment.

We have to look after the burial mounds

As you know, archaeologists work at finding and excavating things from past times. However, the most important job they have is to make very sure that the

The highways agency was due to build a better road past Gulli. The archaeologists therefore had to excavate the cemetery before it was destroyed. In the burial mound in the centre, the dead person had been laid in a boat.

objects, buildings and graves are carefully looked after. The burial mounds of the Viking Age have been there for a thousand years. In Norway, it has been decided that those who live after us should also be able to experience what it is like to walk through a Viking-age cemetery. For this reason, there is a law that protects cemeteries, settlements and all objects that date from before 1537. This is called the Cultural Heritage Act.

This is what archaeologists think that the grave of one of the women at Gulli looked like. She was buried with two brooches, three glass beads, a fine pin, a sickle, shears, a spindle, a horse's head and possibly other objects of wood or cloth, which have rotted away.

Slaughtering for Yule

"Today we are going to do the slaughtering for Yule," says Uncle Bjørn. "Two pigs and one cow," he adds.

Thora sees tears come into Ravn's eyes. No great surprise, she thinks; he's so fond of every single animal on the farm. As for herself, she's delighted! Of course she's seen animals being slaughtered in the town, but she's never been able to take part herself.

"You can be my helper, Thora," says Aunt Ingrid. "We shall start with the pigs, and then we need a lot of hot water. You and Ravn can fill these barrels with snow."

Ravn is given the job of going with the first pig to the slaughtering place. The slave grasps the pig and Uncle Bjørn strikes it hard on the head. Then he stabs a hole in the animal's throat and Aunt Ingrid moves like lightning to catch the blood in a wooden bowl.

When the blood stops running, she puts some pieces of ice into the bowl and asks Thora to stir it.

"Do that and the blood won't clot," she says.

Thora's mouth waters at the thought of the fine black puddings they will be making.

Then the slave woman comes up carrying the large iron cauldron. It is full of hot water, which she pours over the dead pig.

"That's to loosen the bristles," says Aunt Ingrid.

The slaves scrape off the bristles. Finally they hang the pig up so that they can take the innards out.

Meanwhile, Ravn has fetched the second pig, but this time it doesn't go so smoothly. The pig shrieks and tries to escape several times before it reaches the slaughtering place.

Thora has the job of stirring the blood again. She looks for Ravn and catches sight of him just as he slips into the byre. Clearly, he needs to enjoy being with the animals that have been allowed to stay alive.

Facts

Home slaughtering

There were no slaughterhouses in the Viking Age, so the animals were killed at the farms themselves. The slaughtering usually took place in the autumn and early in the winter so that the farmers did not have to feed all of the animals through the winter. Exactly how the slaughtering was carried out we can only guess, but it must have been important to keep as much of the animal as possible. The intestines, for instance, were used as sausage skins.

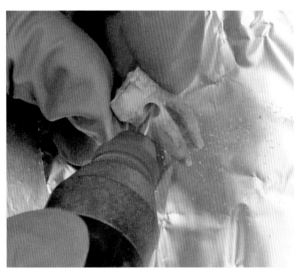

An archaeologist drills out a sample from a tooth from the Viking Age.

Fresh meat for a feast

People ate fresh meat when it had been butchered, but for much of the year there was only dried and salted meat to be had. As a result, there was slaughtering for the great festivals. Fresh meat was what people longed for. We understand this when we read the stories Snorri Sturluson wrote down. We learn that people believed that warriors who died in battle went to Valhalla. In this feasting hall there was fresh meat every single evening. A pig called Sæhrímnir was slaughtered every day, but the next day it was as good as new and could be slaughtered all over again.

You are what you eat

Information on what you have been eating is stored in your skeleton and your teeth. Scientists can find this out by using a new method called isotope analysis. If scientists had been able to examine a small piece of your tooth or one of your bones they could have discovered whether you mostly ate fish,

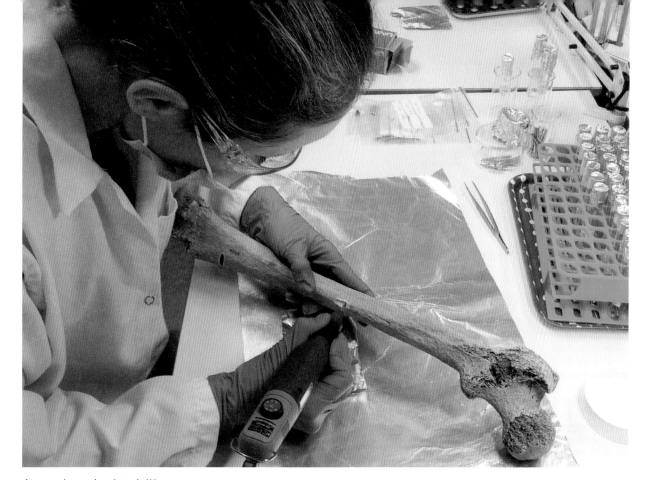

An archaeologist drills out a sample from a leg bone.

vegetables or meat. In the same way, when archaeologists find skeletal remains from the Viking Age, they can investigate what people were eating then.

Our skeletons change throughout our lives and so only provide information on what people were eating in the last years of their lives. Teeth, however, do not change after they have grown to full size. As a result, they tell us about what a person ate as a child.

Children ate less fish

Archaeologists have not yet been able to examine very many skeletons and teeth in this way, as this method is very new. However, they have undertaken such analyses on finds from a cemetery at Flakstad in Nordland. These showed that many people had a different diet when they were children to that which they had later in life. They ate a lot more fish after they had grown up. Archaeologists are wondering how to explain this difference. Were children not allowed to eat fish? Or did the children just not want to eat fish?

Out of chests and boxes

At last, the day on which the Yule Sacrifice would take place had come! Thora was really looking forward to all the lovely food. But first, they all had to bathe and put on their finest clothes.

"We need more water," says Aunt Ingrid, and she sends the children out to fetch some snow. Thora is the quickest at filling the bucket up and she sidles up to Ravn. She tips the lot over his head. He squeals like a pig and runs round in circles trying to shake off the cold snow. Thora is doubled up with laughter and they go on playing around and laughing while they run to and from the slave woman with the buckets.

While the slave woman is heating the water over the fire, Aunt Ingrid and Thora's mother fetch the chests with the fine clothing. Thora gets the first bath and enjoys the lovely warm water, but it's not long before her mother orders her out and it's Ravn's turn to bathe. Then they put on their best clothes while Sigrid and the adults have their baths.

Then the moment comes that Thora has been waiting for. Her mother and Aunt Ingrid unlock the most splendid box. In there are all the most beautiful pieces of jewellery.

"Here's your necklace," says mother, passing it to Thora.

"But wait," says Aunt Ingrid, and she unfastens a large bead from her unbelievably long string of beads. "Your grandmother owned this bead and I want you to have it."

Thora looks at the beautiful bead and quickly threads it on to her necklace. Then Aunt Ingrid picks out the necklace and bracelets she is going to wear herself. They are of clear, shining silver and are some of the most beautiful things Thora has ever seen.

"These were part of my marriage gift," Aunt Ingrid explains.

Facts

Clean Vikings

An English historian who was living in the thirteenth century explained why the Vikings were so popular with English ladies. They took a bath every Saturday, brushed their hair and dressed smartly. This agrees closely with the fact that archaeologists have found a lot of combs, nail-cleaners and tweezers. We also know that both women and men used eye make-up. This is reported by the Spanish-Arabic Jew Al-Tartushi, who visited the Danish Viking-age town of Hedeby in the 10th century.

Buried in their best clothes

The dead were buried fully dressed, and many were dressed in very fine clothing and wore jewellery. Because of this, archaeologists know quite a lot about what people of the Viking Age looked like when they had made themselves smart.

Inherited jewellery

Many necklaces include mixtures of beads of very different ages. The reason may be that women collected beads throughout their lives. They may also have inherited items of jewellery from their mothers and grandmothers. In one grave at the Viking-age town of Birka in Sweden there was a woman who was decked with many kinds of jewellery. Archaeologists have discovered that two of the brooches were a hundred years old when she was buried, so they must have been made long before she was born. Very few people lived for more than 60 years.

Five-year-olds found silver jewellery

Three five-year-old children found some items of silver jewellery while they were playing in Tromsø in Norway in 2005. The objects were handed over to Tromsø

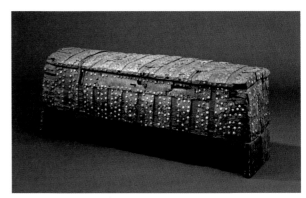

The most valuable objects at the farm were kept in locked boxes or chests.

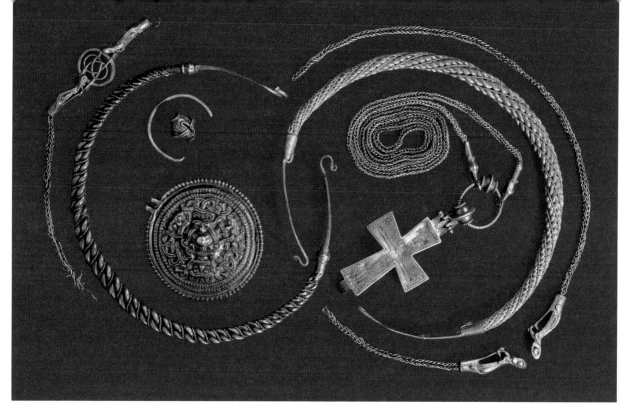

The silver jewellery that was found in Tromsø.

Museum and archaeologists from the museum quickly went out to investigate the site at which they were found. They found more pieces of jewellery, including two silver neckrings from the eleventh century. The children were given a finder's reward from the Directorate of Cultural Heritage and were praised for having handed in what they found, just as one should.

Silver neckrings and bracelets

Archaeologists and other people have often found collections of gold and silver together in a place that is not a grave. These have sometimes been very valuable pieces of jewellery such as neckrings and bracelets. Archaeologists do not agree how they should interpret these finds.

Some think that these are treasure hoards that people had hidden from thieves and pirates but never got to dig up again. Others think that they may have been sacrificed to the gods, because some of the hoards have been found under water, from which it would have been extremely difficult to retrieve them.

Some keys were just as fine as pieces of jewellery.

The Yule Sacrifice

When everyone is ready, they all go together to the cemetery. Aunt Ingrid carries a large bowl of beer, Uncle Bjørn carries a bowl of blood and Ravn is hauling a cauldron of porridge along. Thora wonders whether their ancestors will like the food they have brought.

Uncle Bjørn calls out to the dead and begs them to help the people on the farm in the coming year. Then he sprinkles a little of the blood all around the graves. Aunt Ingrid pours beer into the small wooden bowls by each of the burial mounds and Ravn shares out the porridge.

They return to the house after the ancestors have been given their share of the food and drink. Thora and Ravn are told very firmly that they must keep close to the grown-ups. There are many 'powers' travelling through the air at Yule and not all of them are kind to children.

The inside of the house is decorated for a party, and Aunt Ingrid and Thora's mother bring out tub after tub of the tastiest food: black puddings, cooked meat, roast meat and fat. Then they have to make an offering to the gods. Uncle Bjørn lifts the largest tub aloft and calls upon Thor.

"We ask you to give us a good year – and peace," he says in a serious voice.

Then Aunt Ingrid lifts up the bowl of beer and says, "Give us much corn in the fields and may our animals have many young."

Thora peers into the dark corners to see if she can catch sight of the gods, but it is much too dark.

Aunt Ingrid goes over to a chest and brings out Volsi, who is packed inside many layers of cloth. She calls upon the Giantess and asks her to receive their offering. She passes Volsi on to the other adults and they repeat what she had said. Then the bowl of beer is passed around, with everyone taking a large draught from it. Thora and Ravn take part too and make a toast for a good year and for peace. Then they tuck into the lovely food.

Facts

Celebrating Yule

In the Viking Age, Yule was celebrated at the winter solstice, around the time that Christmas is celebrated nowadays. It was called *jól* or *jólablót*. Specialists are not entirely certain exactly what they celebrated, but we do know that it was important to drink beer and to pray to the gods for a good year and for peace. It was apparently also important to eat together with the gods. The word *blót* means 'sacrifice', and as part of the ceremony of Yule the gods were given some of the meat, fat and blood from an animal that had been slaughtered. Al-Tartushi, see page 46, describes a sacrificial meal of this kind at Hedeby in Denmark. It was a party designed to honour the gods and for eating and drinking.

Yule is made Christian

Christianity was introduced to Scandinavia in the course of the Viking Age, and the kings were amongst the first

At Bergene in Vestfold, Norway, there is a well-preserved cemetery with about 30 burial mounds.

who converted to Christianity. They wanted Christianity to become a popular religion. For that reason they wanted people to continue to hold their parties but that these should have a Christian meaning. The kings decided that *jól* should be about the birth of Jesus Christ.

Living with the dead

People believed that the dead were still present on the farm and that they were living in their graves. Those who were living on the farm could get into contact with their dead relatives by giving them food and drink.

Different gods and powers

In the Viking Age, people believed in a lot of different gods and powers. Some of the gods, such as Odin, Thor and Baldr, were male, while others, such as Freyja and Frigg, were female. There were also 'powers' such as giants, elves, spirits and the Norns.

'The Tale of Volsi'

'The Tale of Volsi' is a story that was written down after the people in Scandinavia had become Christian. It makes fun of the religion of the Viking Age, but still provides information about what people on the farms believed in. It tells us that the leading woman of the farm kept a horse's penis after the stallion had been slaughtered. She packed it away with an onion and wrapped in a piece of cloth; this was 'Volsi'. In the evening she took Volsi out of a chest and begged the Giantess to receive the offering. The Giantess was a wild force of nature, while the stallion was one of the most important of the farm animals. As a result, people may have believed that to give Volsi to the Giantess would lead to a good harvest and many fat animals on the farm.

This is how archaeologists think one of the men at Gulli was buried: with his sword, spear, axe, shield, knife, a soapstone cauldron, a sickle, a box, his whetstone, a weight, a rattle, a bell, several bridles and other horse-gear.

Sigrid's great journey

The day after the Yule Ceremony, Thora and her family were to travel back to Kaupang.

"I cannot be away too long," says her mother. "People might decide to go to other sellers to buy cloth."

Thora notices that Aunt Ingrid is going round with tears in her eyes, and she wonders why. She surely isn't that sad that they have to go?

"It's so nice that Sigrid can travel with you to the town," says Uncle Bjørn suddenly, and Thora pricks her ears up. The grown-ups must have agreed something after she had gone to bed.

"No, it's a pleasure," Thora's mother replies. "That way she'll have company for a good bit of her journey."

Thora looks inquisitively at Ravn, who seems to know what they are talking about. They slip off into a corner and Ravn explains that Sigrid has to go to the great farm of Oseberg to be brought up by their mother's elder sister. This aunt is going to bring Sigrid up to be a fine lady.

"That's important for Sigrid and for our family," Ravn explains. "Aunt Åsa is becoming one of the most powerful people throughout the Viken region."

Sigrid enters the room with her finest box in her arms.

"I have finished packing," she says.

Aunt Ingrid gives her a tight hug and tells her to remember everything she has learnt at home.

Then it is time to say goodbye. Sigrid sits beside Thora in the sleigh and spreads furs over them. Ravn puts his skis on to go some of the way with them. Aunt Ingrid stays standing in the doorway and waves for as long as they are still in sight.

Facts

Foster-children

In the Viking Age, many children left their homes to live with a different family as foster-children. This seems to have been particularly common with rich families. Both boys and girls were sent for fostering. They could be living with their foster-families for years. Håkon, the youngest of King Harald Fairhair's sons, was sent as far away as to England to be fostered by Athelstan the English king. At that time he was about 10 years old. He remained there for many years and afterwards was called Håkon Adelsteinfostre (Athelstan's Foster-son).

Friendships

There was no police force, or anyone else to turn to if someone behaved badly. It was important, therefore, to have a lot of relatives and friends who would help if one ran into problems. Sending children off for fostering was one way of building friendships. The foster-parents were obliged to assist their foster-children on every occasion. The families also had to turn out to support one another if there were fights.

Memorial stones

Parents had to be prepared for their children to die apart from them and nearly all families lost one or more children because of illness. The Icelandic chieftain Egil Skalla-Grímsson composed a long poem after his sons died. A lady called Gunnvor had a stone monument raised in memory of her dead daughter Astrid. On this, it is written that Astrid was the cleverest girl in the whole of Hadeland; Gunnvor must have been proud of her daughter.

The family was important

Memorial stones of this kind are also called rune-stones. The stones have texts inscribed on them in runic letters. These

The memorial stone that was raised by Gunnvor stood at the farm of Dynna at Gran in Oppland, Norway. You can now see it in the the Historical Museum, Oslo.

The memorial stone that was raised by Harald Bluetooth is still standing outside the church at Jelling in Denmark.

texts show how much the family mattered to people. Gunnvor relates that she is the daughter of Thidrik, so that everyone will know who her father was. Surnames were taken from the father's first name, but the families of both the father and the mother were regarded as equally important. The Danish king Harald Bluetooth raised a memorial stone to his parents. On this it is stated that "Harald, the king, ordered this memorial to be made to Gorm his father and Thyra his mother."

More facts

About the Viking Age
Unn Pedersen: *The Viking Town,* Gyldendal, 2016

About archaeology
Kate Duke: *Archaeologists Dig for Clues.* Harper Collins, 1996

Sources for this book

Arne Emil Christensen, Anne Stine Ingstad and Bjørn Myhre: *Osebergdronningens grav. Vår arkeologiske nasjonalskatt i nytt lys.* Schibsted 1992. (The Grave of the Oseberg Queen)

Lars Erik Gjerpe: Gravfeltet på Gulli. Kulturhistorisk museum 2005. (The Cemetery at Gulli)

Elise Naumann, T. Douglas Price and Michael P. Richards: Changes in dietary practices and social organization during the pivotal late Iron Age period in Norway (AD 550-1030): Isotope analyses of Merovingian and Viking Age human remains. *American Journal of Physical Anthropology,* 155:3 (2014), pp.322-331.

Hans Jacob Orning: *Norvegr: Norges historie, bind 1.* Aschehoug, 2011 (Nordvegr: The History of Norway)

Else Roesdahl: *The Vikings.* Penguin 1999.

Jon Vidar Sigurdsson: *Norsk historie 800–1300.* Det Norske Samlaget, 1999. (Norwegian History 800–1300)

Jon Vidar Sigurdsson: *Den vennlige vikingen.* Pax 2010. (The Friendly Viking)

Gro Steinsland: *Norrøn religion. Myter, riter, samfunn.* Pax, 2005. (Norse religion. Myths, Rituals, Society)

Thanks to
Lars Erik Gjerpe; Isak Leirfjord-Pedersen; Inger-Lise Pedersen; Marianne Hem Eriksen; Heidi Berg; Souvenir Normand, British Section; Souvenir Normand, Norwegian Section; John Hines; David Penfold.

Index

* Words that appear repeatedly on many pages are listed only where they appear first.

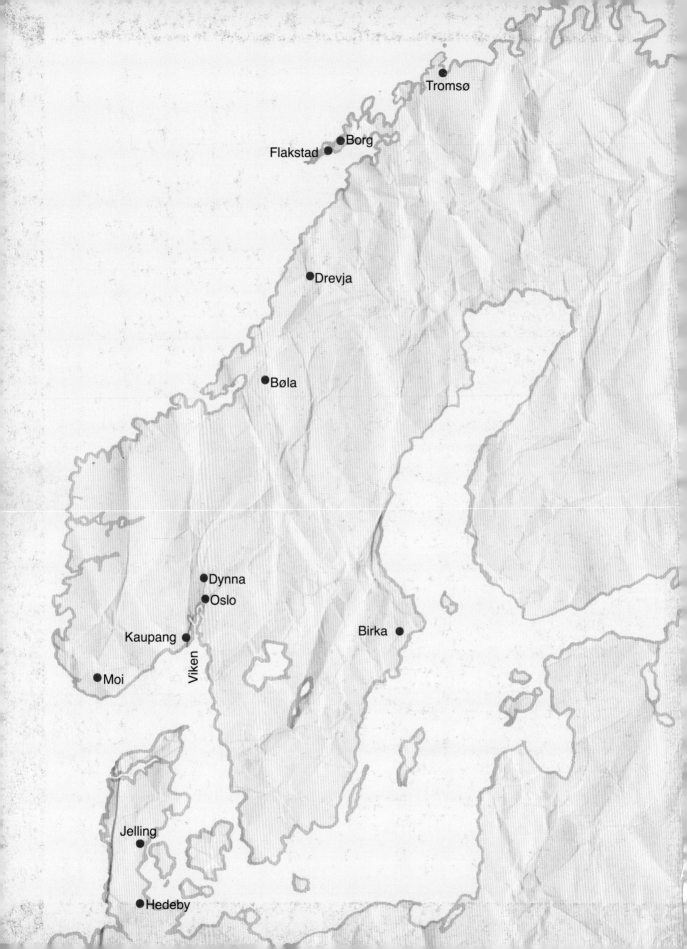

Tromsø

Borg
Flakstad

Drevja

Bøla

Dynna
Oslo
Kaupang
Viken
Moi

Birka

Jelling

Hedeby